This vampire bat belongs to:

To my companions Hero, Remy & Pan xxx – G. D.

To Aleisha Quianna Maglalang – A. B.

First published in 2022 in the United States of America
by Thames & Hudson Inc., 500 Fifth Avenue, New York,
New York 10110

Library of Congress Control Number 2021952536

ISBN 978-0-500-65296-1

Printed and bound in China by Everbest Printing Co. Ltd.

FSC
www.fsc.org
MIX
Paper from
responsible sources
FSC® C124385

Be the first to know about our new releases,
exclusive content and author events by visiting
thamesandhudson.com
thamesandhudsonusa.com
thamesandhudson.com.au

If I had a vampire bat

GABBY DAWNAY   ALEX BARROW

I do like ,

I've got a ,

a (were) would be cool!

But I'd prefer the kind of pet
that I could take to school...

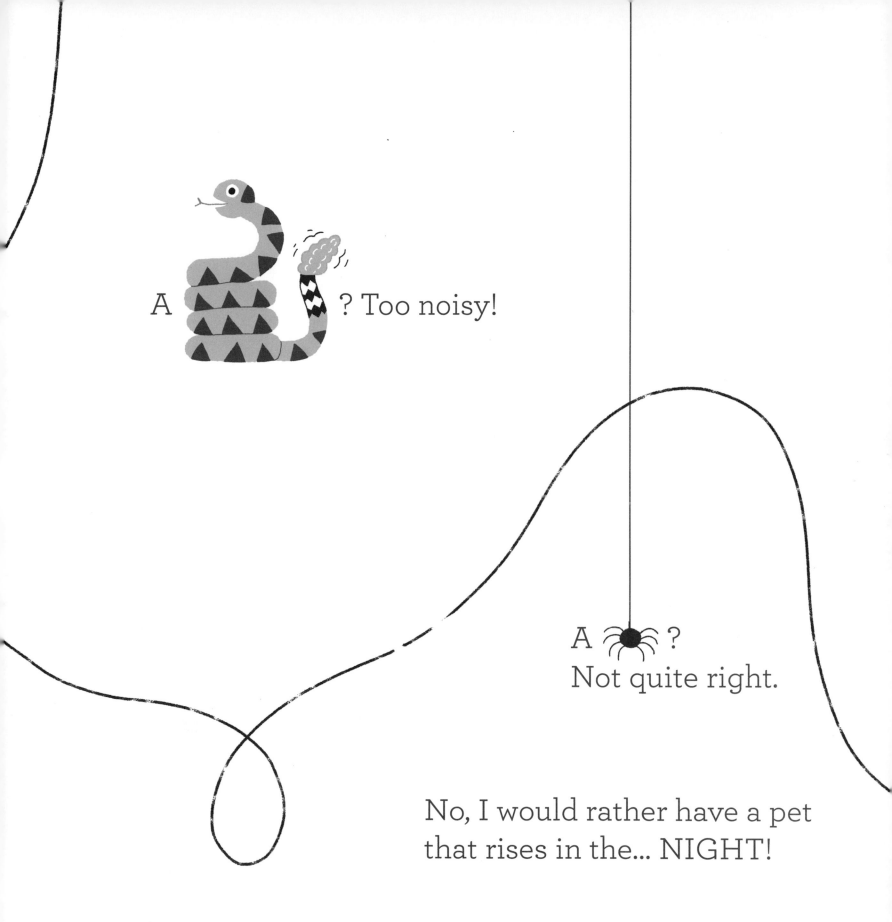

A ? Too noisy!

A ?
Not quite right.

No, I would rather have a pet
that rises in the... NIGHT!

I really want a spooky pet
that flaps around and hangs.
A toothy type of swoopy pet
with shiny pointed fangs...

Oh if I had a...

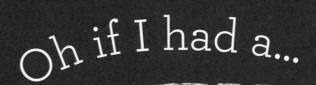

vampire bat

we'd sleep throughout the day
and wait until the moon appeared
to wake again and play!

Vampire bats need lots of blood,
so she would have to munch...

...a large amount for breakfast,
then a jug or two for lunch!

I'd take her to the dentist,
who I guess would get a fright...

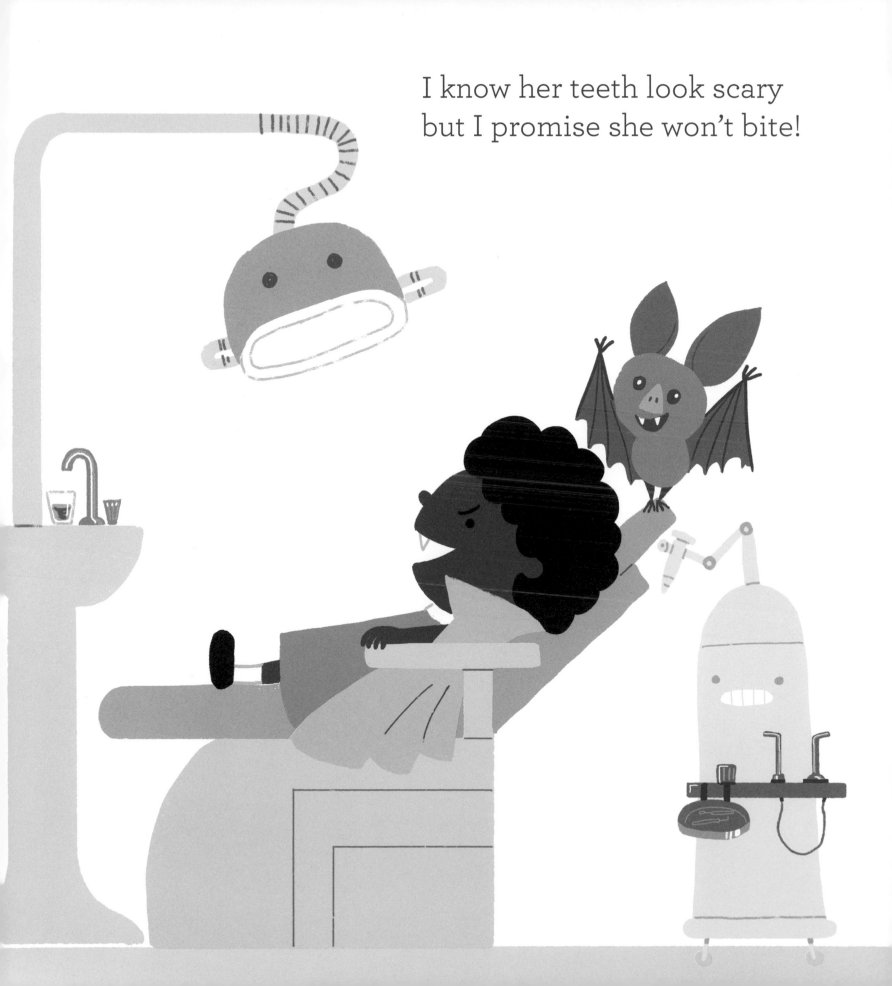

I know her teeth look scary but I promise she won't bite!

If I had a vampire bat
I'd take her to the park,
but only when the sun had set
'cause bats prefer the dark...

Here lies
Sugarsnap
Rest in Peas

This be Boo.
Asleep,
not dead,
dozing in
the flowerbed

Bats have special radar
to help them find their way,
and this would come in handy
for the games we like to play!

Little Monsters School

If the street fair came to town
we'd go on every ride.
The Haunted House is SO much fun,
we'd run to get inside...

Dare you Enter

Every year at Halloween
we'd stroll around the street,
politely asking neighbors
if they wanted "Trick or treat?"

Vampire bats are very kind
because they really care.
So if my bat had more than me,
I know that she would share!

Bats are very flappy—
they flutter high and swoop,
so always wear a witch's hat
and watch out for the...

NO TRICK
OR TREAT!

Vampires love a party
full of music and balloons.

My bat would be the DJ,
playing funky monster tunes!

Every single bedtime
we would have a strict routine,
'cause bats have lots of pointy teeth
and need to keep them clean...

Vampire bats get sleepy
but they do not go to bed...
so we would use my closet
and hang upside down instead!

If I had a vampire bat
the fun would never end...
I WISH I had a vampire bat
as my eternal friend!

Meet the creators of the series

Gabby Dawnay is a writer and poet. She is a regular contributor to *OKIDO* magazine and a scriptwriter for children's television.

Alex Barrow is a London-based illustrator and musician. He is the art director for and a regular contributor to *OKIDO* magazine.

Together Gabby and Alex are the duo behind the bestselling *If I had a* series, as well as numerous other children's books including *A House for Mouse* and *A Song for Bear* (both Thames & Hudson).